City Sounds

Written by Jean Marzollo

Illustrated by Sophia Latto

SCHOLASTIC INC.

New York   Toronto   London   Auckland   Sydney

"City Sounds" by Jean Marzollo
from *Let's Find Out*, January 1976.
Text Copyright © 1976, 1994 by Scholastic Inc.
Illustrations Copyright © 1994 by Scholastic Inc.
All rights reserved. Published by Scholastic Inc.
Printed in the U.S.A.
ISBN 0-590-27563-1

3 4 5 6 7 8 9 10   08   00 99 98 97 96 95 94

Maryanne and her grandfather were sitting on a park bench.

"What is your favorite sound?" asked Grandpa.

Maryanne thought for a while and then said,
"Well, I like car sounds,

BEEP BEEP

and motorcycle sounds,

VVRROOOOMM

and cats that meow at night,

MEOW

and fire engine sirens,

AARRRRRRRRR

and noisy buses,

BRUMMM

and pigeons in the park,

coooo coooo

and police whistles,

TWEEET

and honking trucks,

HONK HONK

and footsteps on the stairs,

CLIP CLOP

and dogs barking outside."

WOOF WOOF

Maryanne said, "Grandpa, I like lots of sounds. Why do you want to know which one is my favorite?"

"Because I was hoping you'd say this sound," said Grandpa. And with that, he pulled out his harmonica and played a happy tune.

"Oh, Grandpa, you've been teasing me. That's not a sound. That's the best music in the whole wide world."